MARY-MARY

'Mary-Mary is delicious—the "baby" of the family who gets in the way of her bigger brothers and sisters but more than manages to hold her own.'

Times Literary Supplement

'A nuisance to her brothers and sisters, a problem to her mother and an enigma to her neighbours, Mary-Mary is the most enchanting child whose adventures always turn out in an unexpectedly happy manner. The author writes in just the kind of way and about just the kind of things that will interest, and intrigue the very young.'

Birmingham Post

Lovely stories for six year olds and upwards to enjoy.

MARY-MARY

Written and Illustrated by

JOAN G. ROBINSON

COLLINS · LIONS

First published 1957 by George G. Harrap & Co Ltd
First published in Lions 1972
by William Collins Sons and Co Ltd
14 St James's Place, London SW1
Second Impression September 1972
Third Impression June 1974

© Joan G. Robinson 1957

Printed in Great Britain
by William Collins Sons and Co Ltd, Glasgow

Contents

For
Susanna

ONE

Mary-Mary goes Visiting

Once upon a time there was a little girl called Mary-Mary.

She was the youngest of five, and all her brothers and sisters were very big and clever, and knew all about everything. Mary-Mary didn't know much about anything; so all her big brothers and sisters, who were called Miriam, Martyn, Mervyn, and Meg, used to say to her, 'Don't do it like that, Mary-Mary. Do it like this!' or 'Don't go that way, Mary-Mary. Come this way!'

Then Mary-Mary would say, 'No. I shall do it my own way,' and, 'No. I am going the other way.'

And that, of course, is why she was called Mary-Mary instead of just Mary, which was her real name.

One day Mary-Mary started coming downstairs backwards, pulling a box of bricks behind her.

Miriam, Martyn, Mervyn, and Meg were all standing together in the hall, and when they heard Mary-Mary coming *bumpety-bump* down

'Don't come down backward, Mary-Mary. You'll fall down!'

the stairs backwards they all started shouting at her at once:

'Don't come down backwards, Mary-Mary. You'll fall down!'

Mary-Mary fell down. And all the bricks came after her.

'There!' said Miriam. 'We said you'd fall down.'

'There!' said Martyn. 'We knew you would.'

'There!' said Mervyn. 'Just as we said.'

'There!' said Meg. 'What did we tell you?'

'You told me to fall down,' said Mary-Mary, 'and I think it was very silly of you.'

She sat on the bottom stair and looked to see which of her legs was broken. Neither of them was, so she picked up her box of bricks and sat them in her lap. She wasn't really hurt, only surprised.

Mother ran out of the kitchen.

'What was that bump?' she said.

'My bricks fell down and I'm nursing them better,' said Mary-Mary.

All the others started talking to Mother at once. They were all wanting to do different things.

'Can I go round to Barbara's house?' said Miriam. 'She wants to show me the new kitten.'

'Can I go fishing with Billy?' said Martyn. 'He's got a new fishing-line, and I can use his old one.'

'Can I go and play with Bob?' said Mervyn. 'He's got a new electric train.'

Mother put her hands over her ears and said, 'Please, please, don't all talk at once. Yes, Miriam, you can go to Barbara's. But be back in time for tea. Yes, Martyn, you can go fishing with Billy. But do be careful. Yes, Mervyn, you can go and play with Bob. But don't break his new train. Yes, Meg—what do you want?'

'Can I go shopping with Bunty?' said Meg. 'She wants me to help her choose a present.'

'Oh, yes,' said Mother. 'That will be nice for you, especially as all the others have been asked out too—all except Mary-Mary, of course.'

'Why "except me, of course"?' said Mary-Mary. 'Why doesn't anyone ask me out?'

'Oh, but they do,' said Mother. 'You and I quite often get asked out, don't we?'

'By myself, I mean,' said Mary-Mary.

'Don't be silly,' said Miriam.

'You're not old enough,' said Martyn.

'You couldn't go alone,' said Mervyn.

'You're too little,' said Meg.

Then they all said, 'Never mind, Mary-Mary,' together, and went off to get ready.

Mary-Mary dragged her box of bricks out into the garden, talking to herself loudly all the way.

'When I'm a lady,' she said, 'I shall have lots and lots of children, but they'll all be exactly the same age. I won't have even one a little bit older than the others.'

She began building a little house out of bricks for Moppet, her pet mouse.

Moppet was a toy mouse, with a key to wind

him up, but he looked very real and was quite good for frightening people with if they didn't already know him.

Mary-Mary wrapped him in her handkerchief and put him down to sleep inside the little brick house.

'There you are, my pet,' she said. 'What you would do without me to look after you I just don't know. Now go to sleep, and when you're bigger I may let you go out visiting all by yourself.'

Then she dragged the brick box close to the garden wall and climbed up on to it so that she could see over the other side.

Miriam, Martyn, Mervyn, and Meg were all tall enough to see over the wall into the next-door garden if they stood on tiptoe, but Mary-Mary couldn't. She was too little.

Just then Miriam came running out on her way to Barbara's house.

'Good-bye, Mary-Mary,' she said. 'Don't look over the wall. It's rude.'

'Good-bye,' said Mary-Mary. But she stayed where she was.

Then Martyn came running out on his way to go fishing with Billy.

'Good-bye, Mary-Mary,' he said. 'Don't stare over the wall.'

'Good-bye,' said Mary-Mary, still standing on the box.

Then Mervyn ran out on his way to play with Bob.

'Good-bye, Mary-Mary,' he said. 'You'd better get down off that box.'

'Good-bye,' said Mary-Mary. But she still stayed where she was.

Then Meg ran out on her way to go shopping with Bunty.

'Good-bye, Mary-Mary,' she said. 'Don't stand on that box. And don't stare over the wall. It's rude. Anyway, you'll fall.'

Mary-Mary fell, and by the time she had picked herself up again Meg had gone.

'Bother that girl,' said Mary-Mary. 'She's always making me fall down.'

She peeped into the little brick house. Moppet's beady black eye was showing over the top of the handkerchief blanket. Mary-Mary brought him out, unwrapped him, and put him on top of the wall. Then she kicked down the little brick house and shouted in Moppet's voice, 'Don't kick the house down. It's rude.' After that she walked once round the garden, then came back to Moppet, who was still sitting on the wall where she had left him.

'Moppet,' said Mary-Mary sweetly, 'you

mustn't stare over the wall. It's rude. Anyway, you'll fall.'

Then, quite by mistake, she gave him a little push with her hand, and he fell over the other side of the wall into the next-door garden.

Mary-Mary climbed up on the brick box and looked over the wall. But she couldn't see Moppet. He had fallen into the flower-bed and was too far down for her to see.

'Alas, poor Moppet,' said Mary-Mary, and she got down and began walking round and round the garden, wondering how she was going to get him back again.

In a minute she heard the sound of a door opening, and then of footsteps in the next-door garden. Soon she saw the top of a large straw hat moving along behind the wall.

She climbed up on the box again. The large straw hat was just below her on the other side.

Mary-Mary made a little humming noise. The hat looked up, and there was a lady's face underneath it.

'Hallo,' said the lady under the hat.

'Hallo,' said Mary-Mary.

'How big you are!' said the lady. 'Fancy being able to see over the top of the wall!'

'Yes,' said Mary-Mary, 'I am quite big.' She thought for a minute and then she said, 'But I'm

The hat was just below her on the other side

not quite as big as this really. I'm standing on a box.'

'Oh, I see,' said the lady. 'And what is your name?'

'I'm Mary-Mary. Who are you?'

'I'm Miss Summers. I'm your new neighbour. I've only been living here a few weeks.'

'I've been living here for years and years,' said Mary-Mary, 'so I suppose I'm your old neighbour. Just now I'm looking for my mouse.'

Then she told Miss Summers how Moppet had fallen over the wall.

Miss Summers looked all along the flower bed, but she couldn't see Moppet.

'He must be somewhere,' she said. 'Perhaps one of your big brothers and sisters would like to come over and see if they can find him?'

'They are all out,' said Mary-Mary. And she told Miss Summers all about how Miriam had gone to Barbara's house and Martyn had gone fishing with Billy and Mervyn had gone to play with Bob and Meg had gone shopping with Bunty, and how she had to stay at home until she was big enough to be asked out by herself.

'Well, then,' said Miss Summers, 'would you like to come? I wonder if I could lift you over the wall.'

'If you would like me to come as a proper visitor I would come round to the front door,' said Mary-Mary.

Miss Summers thought that would be a good idea.

'Yes, do come as a proper visitor,' she said.

So Mary-Mary ran indoors, and along the passage to the front door. The front-door handle was rather high, but she could easily reach it if she jumped. Mary-Mary held on to the net curtain that hung over the glass part of the door, and jumped. Something snapped and the curtain fell to the floor.

Mary-Mary picked it up, put it round her shoulders, and looked in the hall mirror. She

nodded at herself and said, 'Good afternoon. I
believe you are expecting me?' Then she went
out, shut the door behind her, and walked
slowly and politely round to the front of the
next-door house.

Miss Summers opened the door at once.

'Good afternoon,' said Mary-Mary. 'I believe you are expecting me?'

'Oh, yes,' said Miss Summers. 'Good afternoon. Do come in. How nice of you to come.'

'That's right,' said Mary-Mary. 'I'm glad
you knew what I meant about being a proper
visitor.'

They went in. It was a very grown-up house
with no toys anywhere, but there was a cuckoo
clock in the hall and a rocking-chair in the
sitting-room, and in the kitchen, when they
looked inside the door, Mary-Mary saw a plate
of little pink cakes on the table.

'These look pretty,' she said.

'Yes,' said Miss Summers. 'I've just finished
making them. We will have them for tea.'

When Mary-Mary had rocked in the rocking-
chair, played the piano, and seen the cuckoo
come out twice, she went out into the garden,
and there she found Moppet standing on his
head under a hollyhock.

Miss Summers brought out two deck-chairs

"Good afternoon. I believe you are expecting me?"

and a little table, and put them in the middle of the lawn.

'We will have tea out here, as it's so nice and sunny,' she said. And she found a real lady's sunshade (which she didn't need herself, because she had her large straw hat), and lent it to Mary-Mary. Then she went indoors to put the kettle on.

Mary-Mary sat in the long deck-chair, with the net curtain round her shoulders and the real lady's sunshade over her head, and felt like a very proper visitor.

—smiled secretly to herself and closed her eyes

When Miriam and Martyn and Mervyn and Meg came home they couldn't see Mary-Mary anywhere. They looked all over the house and all round the garden, but she was nowhere to be seen. Then they saw her brick box still standing by the wall.

'She couldn't have gone over, could she?' said Miriam.

'Oh, no,' said Martyn, 'she's not big enough.'

'She wouldn't dare,' said Mervyn. 'It's too high.'

"Whatever are you doing there?"

'Let's just look and make sure,' said Meg.

So they all stood in a row on tiptoe and looked over the wall into the next-door garden. And there what should they see but Mary-Mary sitting in a deck-chair with a little table by her side and a sunshade over her head!

'Mary-Mary!' they all said together. 'Whatever are you doing there?'

Mary-Mary smiled secretly to herself and closed her eyes. It was very pleasant to be sitting in the sun like a grown-up lady.

Miriam and Martyn and Mervyn and Meg all started whispering together on the other side of the wall.

'Oh, isn't she naughty!'

'She's got over the wall.'

'She's sitting in the next-door garden.'

'Just as if she belonged there.'

There was more whispering and rustling, and then the four heads appeared over the top of the wall again.

'Come back at once, Mary-Mary,' said Miriam.

'Or we'll tell Mother,' said Martyn.

'Some one might see you,' said Mervyn.

'Hurry,' said Meg.

Mary-Mary turned round slowly and smiled at them all like a very beautiful lady.

'You mustn't look over the wall,' she said. 'It's rude.'

Just then Miss Summers came out of the house carrying a tea-tray with two cups and saucers and the plateful of little pink cakes.

Miriam and Martyn and Mervyn and Meg all bobbed down behind the wall when they saw her coming, but Mary-Mary could hear them whispering together.

'Perhaps she was invited.'

'She couldn't have been!'

'I wonder if Mother knows.'

'I can't believe it.'

When Miss Summers had put the tray down on the table Mary-Mary said, 'Did you see a

row of children with rather dirty faces looking
over the wall just now?'

Miss Summers smiled.

'Yes, I thought I did,' she said. 'Were they
your brothers and sisters?'

'I'm afraid so,' said Mary-Mary. 'They
shouldn't have stared over the wall like that.
I'm always telling them not to. But I'm sure
they didn't mean to be so rude.'

'Oh, I'm sure they didn't,' said Miss Summers. 'Now, do help yourself to a pink cake,
won't you? Take two, as they're so small.'

So Mary-Mary went visiting by herself after all,
and that is the end of the story.

TWO

Mary-Mary earns some Money

One day Mary-Mary saw all her big brothers and sisters coming out of the kitchen looking very busy and important. Miriam had a bucket of water and a scrubbing-brush, Martyn had a broom, Mervyn had a set of shoe-brushes, and Meg had a packet of soap powder.

'What are you all going to do?' said Mary-Mary.

'Don't worry us now,' said Miriam.

'We're busy,' said Martyn.

'We're going to do some work,' said Mervyn.

'And earn some money,' said Meg.

Mary-Mary looked at the bucket of water, the packet of soap powder, and all the different kinds of brushes, and thought they looked interesting.

'I'll come too,' she said.

But all the others turned round together and said, 'Oh, no, Mary-Mary—not you! Now do go away.'

So, of course, Mary-Mary followed them.

Miriam went to the back-door step and began scrubbing it. Mary-Mary watched her and

— so, of course, Mary-Mary followed them

thought it looked rather fun to dip the brush in
the bucket like that and slosh water all over the
step.

'Are you going to get money for doing that?'
she asked, rather surprised.

'Yes,' said Miriam. 'Threepence. When
you're as big as me you'll be able to earn threepence too.'

'I'll do it now,' said Mary-Mary, reaching
for the brush.

'Oh, no, you won't,' said Miriam. 'You'll
upset the bucket.'

Mary-Mary stepped backwards and sat in the
bucket by mistake. It upset.

'Now look what you've done,' said Miriam.

'I don't need to look,' said Mary-Mary. 'I
can feel it. That water was very wet.'

"Are you going to get money for doing that?"

Miriam went off to fill the bucket with more water, and Mary-Mary, with her skirt all wet and dripping, went away to see what the others were doing.

Martyn was sweeping up the mess round the dustbins.

'Will you get threepence for doing that?' asked Mary-Mary.

'Yes,' said Martyn; 'so can you when you're as big as me.'

'I'll start now,' said Mary-Mary, reaching for the broom.

'No, you're not big enough,' said Martyn. 'You'd make yourself dirty.'

Mary-Mary stepped backwards and tripped over a pile of dust and tea-leaves. It flew up all round her, and as she was wet it stuck to her in quite a lot of places.

'I seem to have got rather dirty,' she said.

'I knew you would,' said Martyn, and he started sweeping it up all over again.

So Mary-Mary, with her skirt all wet and dripping, and covered with dust and tea-leaves, went away to see what the others were doing.

Mervyn was kneeling on the garden step polishing shoes. Mary-Mary stood and watched for a while. Two tins of polish lay open on the step, one very black and the other shiny brown. Mervyn dipped one brush into the polish and put it on the shoes, then he rubbed them with another brush and polished them with a soft cloth until they shone.

'Do you like doing that?' asked Mary-Mary.

'Not much,' said Mervyn, 'but I'll get three-pence for it.'

Mary-Mary knelt down on the step beside him.

'Now I'll do some,' she said.

'No, you won't,' said Mervyn. 'You'll only get covered in polish. Get up, now.'

Mary-Mary got up, and the two tins of polish were stuck to her knees. She hadn't looked where she was kneeling, and the very black one was stuck to her right knee, and the shiny brown one was stuck to her left knee. She took them off quickly before Mervyn noticed. He was polishing hard.

'When you're as big as me you'll be able to earn threepence, too,' he said. 'Now do go away. You'll only get covered in polish.'

Mary-Mary looked at her knees.

'I am already,' she said, and rubbed some of it off on to her hands.

So Mary-Mary, with her skirt all wet and dripping, covered with dust and tea-leaves, and with shoe-polish on her hands and knees, went away to see what Meg was doing.

Meg was in the garden washing her dolls' blankets in a bowl.

'Why are you doing that?' said Mary-Mary.

'They were very dirty,' said Meg, 'and if I wash all the dolls' clothes as well I'm going to get threepence.'

Mary-Mary picked up the packet of soap powder.

'I'll do some washing too,' she said. 'I'd like to earn threepence.'

'You can't,' said Meg. 'You're too little. Wait till you're as big as me and then you can. Put down that packet—you'll spill it.'

"You're spilling it!"

But Mary-Mary held the packet high above her head and wouldn't put it down.

'You're spilling it!' shouted Meg. 'You've got it upside down. It's running all over your hair.'

Mary-Mary put it down again.

'I wondered what was tickling my head,' she said.

'Go away now,' said Meg.

'No,' said Mary-Mary, and stayed where she was.

'Oh, well, then—stay if you must,' said Meg.

'No, I won't,' said Mary-Mary. 'I'm going away.'

So Mary-Mary, with her skirt all wet and dripping, covered with dust and tea-leaves, with shoe-polish on her hands and knees, and soap powder all over her head, went round to the front gate to see if anyone else might be doing anything interesting.

A cat was sitting washing itself on the wall outside. Mary-Mary opened the gate, stroked the cat, and looked around.

The coal cart was standing a few doors away, outside Mr Bassett's house. The coalman wasn't there, but Mr Bassett was walking round and round the cart talking to himself. Every now and then he stooped down and tried to look underneath it, but he was a big, fat man, and it was difficult for him to bend easily in the middle.

Mary-Mary wondered what he was doing, and who he was talking to. The coalman's horse was eating out of a nosebag and didn't seem to be taking any notice of him.

Mary-Mary moved a little nearer.

Mr Basset straightened his back, looked at the horse with a worried face, and said, 'Puss, puss.'

'It isn't a cat. It's a horse,' said Mary-Mary.

Mr Bassett turned and saw her.

'Ah, Mary-Mary!' he said. 'You're a much better size than I am. Do you mind looking under the coal cart and telling me what you can see there?'

Mary-Mary bent down.

'I can see a lump of coal,' she said.

'Anything else?' said Mr Bassett.

'Yes,' said Mary-Mary, 'quite a lot of things. There's another lump of coal and a silver pencil and a piece of paper——'

'Isn't there a cat there?' asked Mr Bassett.

'No,' said Mary-Mary.

'Are you sure?' said Mr Bassett.

'Yes, quite sure,' said Mary-Mary, 'but there's a cat sitting on the wall over there if you really want one.'

Mr Bassett looked up and saw the cat washing itself on the wall.

'Well I never!' he said. 'It must have run out when I wasn't looking. I saw it go under the cart as I came out of the gate, and I was afraid it might get run over when the coalman came back. I bent down to call it out, but it wouldn't come. Then I felt something fall out of my pocket, but I was more worried about the cat.'

Mary-Mary liked Mr Bassett. It was kind of him to be so worried about the cat.

'Shall I fetch out what you dropped?' she

asked. 'I can get under the cart more easily than you can.'

'Won't you get dirty?'

Mary-Mary looked down at herself.

'I don't think I could get much dirtier than I am,' she said.

'No, perhaps not,' said Mr Bassett. 'It's very kind of you.'

So Mary-Mary crawled underneath the back of the coal cart, and Mr Basset stood by waiting.

'Oh!' called Mary-Mary, 'there's half a crown down here as well!'

'Good,' said Mr Bassett. 'Bring out everything you see. I can't be quite sure what fell out of my pocket.'

So Mary-Mary picked up the half-crown and the two lumps of coal and the piece of paper and the silver pencil, and crawled out again.

'Good girl,' said Mr Bassett. 'Now let's sort them out. These two lumps of coal belong to the coalman, so we'll throw them back on the cart, and the silver pencil belongs to me, so I'll put it in my pocket. The paper doesn't belong to anybody, so we'll throw it away, and the half-crown—well—I think the half-crown belongs to you, because you've earned it.'

'How did I earn it?' said Mary-Mary.

'By being just the right size to fetch it out,'

said Mr Bassett. 'What would you like to spend it on?'

Mary-Mary said, 'I've been thinking all the morning that if I had threepence I'd spend it on an ice lolly.'

Mr Bassett began counting on his fingers.

'We could buy ten ice lollies with this half-crown,' he said, 'but I think that's too many, don't you? Let's go and spend it, anyway. Shall we go to that nice little teashop on the corner?'

'Oh, yes,' said Mary-Mary. 'I'd like to go there very much. That's where I go to watch the ladies sitting in the window drinking their coffee. It's next to the ice-lolly shop. I've always wanted to look like one of those ladies.'

'Very well,' said Mr Bassett, 'so you shall.'

Mary-Mary looked down at herself.

'I'm rather dirty to look like a lady,' she said.

'And I'm rather fat, and don't look like a lady, either,' said Mr Bassett. 'But if we feel right and behave right I don't suppose anyone will notice what we look like. You don't shout and throw things about, do you?'

'Not usually,' said Mary-Mary.

'Or lick your plate?'

'Not when I'm out,' said Mary-Mary.

'Nor do I,' said Mr Bassett, 'so we ought to be all right.'

So Mary-Mary, with her skirt still rather damp, decorated with dust and tea-leaves, with shoe-polish on her hands and knees, soap powder all over her hair, and a smudge of coal-dust on the end of her nose, went walking politely down the road with Mr Bassett to the nice little teashop.

'We will order one very large ice-cream sundae, and one cup of tea,' said Mr Bassett.

'Which will be for which?' asked Mary-Mary politely.

'I shall order the ice-cream sundae for myself,' said Mr Bassett, 'because I like ice-cream sundaes very much. But I am not allowed to eat them, because they make me too fat, so you shall eat it for me and I shall watch you.'

'I don't like tea very much,' said Mary-Mary.

'Then I shall drink it for you,' said Mr Bassett, 'and we shall suit each other very nicely.'

When Miriam and Martyn and Mervyn and Meg had finished washing the doorstep, sweeping round the dustbins, polishing the shoes, and washing the clothes they were all very hot and tired.

'What shall we spend our threepences on?' said Miriam.

'Something cool,' said Martyn.

'Ice lollies,' said Mervyn.

'Good idea,' said Meg.

'But you'd better tidy yourselves up before you go out,' said Mother.

So Miriam and Martyn and Mervyn and Meg washed their hands and brushed their hair, and then they all set off together to buy their ice lollies.

Miriam chose a raspberry flavour, Martyn chose a strawberry, Mervyn chose an orange one, and Meg chose a lime.

Then they all stood in a row, sucking them, and looked into the window of the nice little tea-shop. And suddenly they all opened their eyes very wide and said, 'Look!' all together, for there at the table in the window sat Mary-Mary, looking quite at home, just as if she were a lady drinking her morning coffee; only Mary-Mary wasn't drinking coffee—she was eating a very large ice-cream sundae out of a very tall glass, with a very long spoon.

'It's Mary-Mary!' they all said together.

'With shoe-polish on her hands!'

'And soap powder in her hair!''

'And coal-dust on her nose!''

'And a whacking great ice-cream sundae! Now, however did she get that?'

Mary-Mary waved to them all with the long

They all looked into the window—

spoon and felt very pleased to be sitting on the right side of the window for a change. But Miriam and Martyn and Mervyn and Meg didn't seem to want to wave back to her, so she started talking to Mr Bassett again.

'It's much nicer being on the inside looking out,' she said.

'Nicer than what?' said Mr Bassett.

'Being on the outside looking in,' said Mary-Mary.

'Oh, yes,' said Mr Bassett, 'much nicer.'

—there sat Mary-Mary

He was sitting with his back to the window, so he hadn't seen the others looking in.

'You know, I'm beginning to feel rather sorry for all my brothers and sisters,' Mary-Mary went on.

'Why is that?' said Mr Bassett.

'Well,' said Mary-Mary, 'they earned three-pence each to-day (that's enough to buy an ice lolly), and they kept telling me I could earn threepence too when I was as big as they are. But if *they'd* been only as big as *me* they might have earned half a crown and been sitting in here with us, mightn't they?'

'Yes, I suppose they might,' said Mr Bassett, 'but, of course, there's no need to tell them, unless you want to.'

'Oh, no, I won't tell them,' said Mary-Mary, smiling to herself.

So Mary-Mary did earn some money after all, and that is the end of the story.

THREE

Mary-Mary's Handbag

One day Mary-Mary found a lady's handbag in the dustbin. It was large and flat and shabby, but it opened and shut nicely with a loud snap, and there was a pocket inside which was just the right size for Moppet.

'I'll keep this,' said Mary-Mary. 'It will come in very handy, and I'm sure the dustman won't need it.'

So she took it away and played with it, and opened it and shut it, and put things in it and took them out again, and was very pleased with her find.

'Whatever have you got there?' said Miriam.

'More old rubbish, I expect,' said Martyn.

'Why, it's Mother's old handbag!' said Mervyn.

'The one before last,' said Meg.

Then they all said together, 'Throw it away, Mary-Mary. It's only old rubbish.'

But Mary-Mary said, 'Different things suit different people. A grown-up lady's handbag suits me very well,' and she would not throw it away.

- very pleased with her find

A little later Miriam was out with her friend, Barbara, when she saw Mary-Mary walking down the road with the handbag on her arm.

Oh, dear! thought Miriam. How awful she looks!

'Mary-Mary,' she said, 'if you'll only throw that dreadful old handbag away I'll give you something else.'

'What will you give me?' said Mary-Mary.

Miriam said, 'I'll give you the little basket that my Easter egg was in. It's much prettier than that old thing.'

'All right. When will you give it me?' said Mary-Mary.

'When I come home,' said Miriam. 'I'm just going out with Barbara now, but I'll give it you when I get back. Now go home like a good girl and put that dreadful bag in the dustbin.'

So Mary-Mary went on up the road towards home. Martyn and Mervyn were just coming out of the gate.

'Where are you going?' said Mary-Mary.

'To the sweetshop, to spend our pocket money,' they said.

'I'll come with you,' said Mary-Mary.

'No, not with that awful old handbag,' said Martyn.

'Every one will laugh at you,' said Mervyn.

'*I* don't mind,' said Mary-Mary, walking after them.

'No, but we do,' said Martyn and Mervyn, and they walked even quicker, so that Mary-Mary had to run to keep up.

'Can't you see we want to be by ourselves?' said Martyn.

'All right, I won't interrupt you,' said Mary-Mary.

'Let's pretend we don't know her,' said Mervyn, and they ran on ahead.

When Mary-Mary got to the sweetshop Martyn and Mervyn were standing by the counter waiting to be served. Mary-Mary went

Mary-Mary had to run to keep up

in and stood beside them. They pretended not
to notice her.

A lady in front of them was taking a long time
buying a box of chocolates. After a while Mary-
Mary got tired of waiting and began opening
and shutting her handbag with such loud snaps
that every one looked round to see what the
noise was. Martyn and Mervyn pretended not
to hear.

At last the lady chose her box of chocolates,
and the shopman said, 'That will be ten and
sixpence, please.'

The lady opened her handbag and looked inside.

'I'm afraid I haven't any change,' she said,
and gave the shopman a pound note.

When she had gone the shopman turned to Martyn.

'Are you all together?' he asked.

'No,' said Mary-Mary, 'these boys are by themselves.'

'Then I'll serve you first as you're the smallest,' said the shopman 'What would you like?'

'I'd like two halfpenny chews,' said Mary-Mary.

She opened the dreadful handbag and looked inside. 'But I'm afraid I haven't any change,' she said.

'Now, look here, Mary-Mary,' said Martyn, 'if we buy you two halfpenny chews will you go home and put that awful old thing in the dust-bin?'

'What awful old thing?' said Mary-Mary in a loud, surprised voice. 'Do you mean my hand-bag?'

'Yes,' said Martyn, 'but don't talk so loud.'

'All right,' said Mary-Mary, 'of course I will, if you'll buy me two halfpenny chews.'

'You go on home, then,' said Martyn.

So Mary-Mary went on up the road towards home again. Meg was just coming out of the door as she got there.

'Where are you going?' said Mary-Mary.

'To see my music teacher about the concert on Friday,' said Meg.

'Perhaps I'll come with you,' said Mary-Mary.

'Not with that dreadful old bag,' said Meg. 'Why don't you throw it away? If you'll put it in the dustbin I'll give you my little red purse.'

'Oh, thank you,' said Mary-Mary. And she went indoors, wrapped her dreadful old handbag carefully in newspaper, and put it in the dustbin.

Martyn and Mervyn came home first.

'Where is that old handbag?' they said.

'In the dustbin,' said Mary-Mary.

'Good,' they said, and gave her two half-penny chews. Miriam came home next.

'Did you do as I said?' she asked.

'Yes,' said Mary-Mary.

'Good girl,' said Miriam, and gave her the little basket. Meg came home last.

'Well, is it in the dustbin?' she asked.

'Yes,' said Mary-Mary, 'it's been there a long time.'

'Good,' said Meg, and gave her the little red purse.

Early next morning Mary-Mary saw the dustman coming up the road with his lorry.

Oh, dear! she thought, it would be a pity if

he should throw my handbag in among all the ashes and rubbish. It would spoil it.

She ran out to the dustbin, dug the handbag out from under some potato peelings, and buried it in the sand-pit. Then, when the dustman had gone, she wrapped it up again in fresh news-paper and put it carefully back in the dust-bin.

On the day of the music teacher's concert Miriam, Martyn, Mervyn, and Meg were all waiting to go, when Mother said, 'Where is Mary-Mary? I got her ready first on purpose so that we shouldn't be late. Where can she be?'

'I saw her digging in the sand-pit just now,' said Father, 'but don't you wait. I'll bring her along with me.'

So Miriam, Martyn, Mervyn, and Meg all went off with Mother, and Father followed later with Mary-Mary.

The concert was just going to begin when suddenly there was a loud snap from the back of the hall. Every one looked round, and there was Mary-Mary, smiling brightly, with the dreadful-looking handbag on her arm.

'*Well!*' said Miriam, Martyn, Mervyn, and Meg, all together.

As soon as the concert was over they all ran up to her.

'Didn't I give you a little basket?' said Miriam.

'Didn't we give you two halfpenny chews?' said Martyn and Mervyn.

'Didn't I give you my little red purse?' said Meg.

'Yes. Thank you,' said Mary-Mary, 'and I've got them all in here. This is such a handy hand-bag, it's big enough to hold everything. I've even got Moppet in the pocket. He did enjoy the concert.'

'But you said you'd put it in the dustbin!' they said, all together.

'Yes, and I did,' said Mary-Mary, 'but it was a silly place to keep a handbag. I had to keep washing my hands every time I dug it out, so I don't keep it there any more.'

So Mary-Mary kept her dreadful handbag after all, and that is the end of the story.

FOUR

Mary-Mary goes away

One day Mary-Mary's mother had to go out for the whole afternoon, so Mary-Mary stayed at home with all her big brothers and sisters.

'What are we going to do?' said Mary-Mary. 'Shall we do something nice?'

But Miriam said, 'I know what I'm going to do. I've got to write a letter.'

And Martyn said, 'I know what I'm going to do, too. I'm going to paint a picture.'

Mervyn said, 'I'm going to make a cut-out model.' And Meg said, 'I've got to do my sums. I didn't finish them yesterday, so I've got to do them to-day. It isn't fair, but I suppose I'd better do them, all the same.'

Miriam went into the bedroom to write her letter (because she couldn't think with every one talking to her), and Martyn went into the kitchen (because it was handier for changing the paint water), and Mervyn went into the dining-room (because he needed the table to lay his model out on), and Meg went into the sitting-room (because she said she might as well sit in a comfortable chair, even if she did have to do sums on a Saturday).

Mary-Mary followed them from room to room, but they all said, 'Oh, do go away, Mary-Mary.' 'You're interrupting.' 'Don't be a nuisance.' 'Leave us alone.'

So Mary-Mary went next door to see Miss Summers. But Miss Summers was busy too. She said, 'I'm so sorry, Mary-Mary, but I've no time for visitors to-day, because I'm going away.'

'Where are you going?' asked Mary-Mary.

'To stay with a friend,' said Miss Summers.

'How long for?' asked Mary-Mary.

'I haven't quite decided yet,' said Miss Summers. 'I'll see how I like it. Just now I'm busy getting ready.'

Mary-Mary went home again, and went up to the bedroom.

'Miriam,' she said, 'I won't talk to you while you're writing your letter, but will you tell me when you've finished writing it so that I can talk to you? Because I shan't know how long to go on not interrupting you if you don't tell me when you've finished, and it would be a pity to go on not talking if you had finished, wouldn't it?'

Miriam said, 'Oh, do stop talking, Mary-Mary, and go away!'

So Mary-Mary went down into the kitchen and said, 'Martyn, will you tell me when you've finished painting so that I shall know when I won't be interrupting you?'

But Martyn said, 'Oh, go away, Mary-Mary!'

Then Mary-Mary went into the dining-room.

'Mervyn,' she said, 'I know you haven't finished making your model yet, so I won't interrupt you; but will you tell me when you have finished, because then I shall be able to come and see it without interrupting you, and if I don't know when you've finished I might come and interrupt you without meaning to?'

'You're interrupting me now,' said Mervyn. 'Go away!'

So Mary-Mary went into the sitting-room to see Meg, but before she had time to say a word Meg looked up crossly and said, 'Go *away*, Mary-Mary!' So Mary-Mary went.

'That's funny,' she said to herself. 'They all said the same thing. Every one of them told me to go away.'

She stood in the hall for a minute, thinking hard, then she went next door again.

Miss Summers, in her best hat, was just coming out of the house.

Mary-Mary said, 'Do you mind telling me before you go what you had to do to get ready to go away?'

'Oh, all sorts of things,' said Miss Summers. 'Pack my bag, leave a note for the milkman, lock the back door—why do you want to know?'

'I might be going away myself,' said Mary-Mary, 'and it's useful to know.'

'But you can't go away by yourself until you're grown up,' said Miss Summers.

'Why not?' said Mary-Mary.

'Because little girls can't,' said Miss Summers. 'You'll have to wait till you're a grown-up lady.'

She kissed Mary-Mary good-bye.

'I'll probably be back on Tuesday,' she said, 'then you must come and see me again.'

Mary-Mary went home again, thinking hard all the way.

Miriam was half-way through her letter when the door opened, and Mary-Mary looked in with a tea-cosy on her head.

'Does this look like a lady's hat?' she asked.

Miriam laughed. 'It does rather,' she said.

'Do I look like a grown-up lady?'

'No,' said Miriam, 'you haven't got ladies' shoes on.'

Mary-Mary went away and tried on several pairs of Mother's shoes. They were all rather large.

But I'll soon get used to that, she said to herself.

She chose a pair with high heels, because they made her look taller, and carried them downstairs in her hand. Then she put them on and hobbled into the kitchen where Martyn was still busy painting.

'Do I look like a grown-up lady?' she asked.

Martyn laughed. 'You might if your skirt was longer,' he said.

Mary-Mary slipped the straps of her skirt over her shoulders so that her skirt fell down nearly to her ankles. Then she hobbled away to find Mervyn, who was still busy with his model.

'Do I look like a lady who's going away?' said Mary-Mary.

Mervyn looked up.

'Jolly nearly,' he said, laughing. 'But where's your handbag?'

'Oh, yes—my handbag! I quite forgot!' said Mary-Mary, and she went away and dug it up out of the sand-pit.

Then, with the tea-cosy on her head,

Mother's shoes on her feet, her skirt almost down to her ankles, and her dreadful-looking handbag over her arm, she went off to find Meg.

Meg was still busy with her sums. She was frowning, thinking hard, and counting on her fingers.

'Do I look like a grown-up lady?' asked Mary-Mary.

Meg went on frowning and counting, not looking up.

Mary-Mary asked her again.

'Oh, *go away*!' said Meg.

'Yes. Good-bye,' said Mary-Mary.

Meg looked up, surprised, but Mary-Mary had gone.

She had gone to the cupboard under the stairs to get a paper carrier bag. After that she fetched her toothbrush and a nightie and Moppet. She wrapped them up in a small bundle of comics and put them in the carrier bag.

Then she wrote a note for the milkman. It said, 'Dear Milkman, I've gone away, love from Mary-Mary.' After that she locked the back door. Then she was ready.

She stopped in the hall to say good-bye to herself in the mirror.

'I shall probably be back on Tuesday,' she said.

'Very well, madam,' she answered herself. 'Have a nice time.'

'Thank you,' said Mary-Mary, and stepped out into the street.

— and stepped out into the street

A boy was sitting on the wall on the other side of the road. When he saw Mary-Mary come out of the house wearing her tea-cosy hat, her high-heeled shoes, and with her skirt nearly down to her ankles he stared hard. Then he whistled. Then he laughed out loud.

Mary-Mary took no notice of him and started walking carefully down the road. But her shoes slipped this way and that, and it was difficult not to turn her ankle over, so after a while she stepped out of them and put them in the carrier bag.

The boy got off the wall and followed her down on the other side of the road.

'Where do you think you're going?' he called.

'I'm going away,' said Mary-Mary.

'I don't believe it,' said the boy. 'Where to?'

'To stay with a friend,' said Mary-Mary.

'Yah!' said the boy. 'I don't believe it.'

And he sat down on the wall to watch which way she would go.

Mary-Mary had been in such a hurry to get out without anyone seeing her that she had forgotten to make up her mind where she was going. She began thinking quickly which of her friends she could be going to stay with. Miss Summers had gone away, so it was no good going there. Mrs Merry had no spare bed. Mary-Mary decided that Mr Bassett would be very glad to have her. She turned in at his gate, put on her shoes, and rang the front-door bell.

'I bet you didn't really ring the bell!' shouted the boy.

Mr Bassett's front door opened. Mary-Mary

"I've come to stay with you"

turned round quickly, made a face at the boy,
and stepped inside with a polite cough. Mr
Bassett himself had opened the door.

'Dear me!' he said, looking down at her.
'Where are you going? You look as if you're
going away.'

'Yes, I am. I've come to stay with you,' said
Mary-Mary.

'Are you really? How long for?'

'I haven't quite decided yet. We'll see how I like it, shall we?' said Mary-Mary.

'Dear, dear!' said Mr Bassett. 'Well, you'd better come in.'

He took her into the front room, and Mary-Mary sat on the edge of a large leather arm-chair.

'Would you like to take your hat off?' asked Mr Bassett.

Mary-Mary took it off, and Mr Bassett put it on the sideboard.

'It looks rather like a tea-cosy on there, doesn't it?' said Mary-Mary.

'Yes,' said Mr Bassett, 'I almost thought it was one. Perhaps we'd better hang it on a peg.'

'No, it's all right,' said Mary-Mary, 'don't bother. It can go in this bag with my tooth-brush and nightie.'

'Toothbrush and nightie?' said Mr Bassett. 'Do you mean you're going to sleep here?'

'Yes,' said Mary-Mary.

'But I didn't ask you, did I?'

Mary-Mary thought hard.

'Do people have to be asked before they go away?' she said.

'They do usually.'

'Oh, dear!' said Mary-Mary. 'And I forgot to

ask you to ask me. You'd better ask me now, hadn't you?'

Mr Bassett sat down and wrote her an invitation which said, 'Dear Mary-Mary, Please will you come and stay with me from two to four o'clock to-day. I shall be so pleased if you will.'

'Thank you,' said Mary-Mary. 'I shall like to come very much. But why only till four?'

'I don't like planning things too far ahead,' said Mr Bassett.

'How funny,' said Mary-Mary. 'I like looking forward to things. Never mind—you can write me another invitation at four o'clock asking me to stay till Tuesday. What shall we do now?'

'We could play ludo,' said Mr Bassett. 'Or would you like to come and see my rabbits?'

'Oh, do you keep rabbits?' said Mary-Mary. 'I *am* glad.'

'Yes,' said Mr Bassett, 'and the people next door keep chickens. But I like rabbits better.'

'You're lucky,' said Mary-Mary. 'My father and mother only keep children. I like rabbits better too. Let's go and see them first, and we can play ludo after. That will be very nice.'

So Mary-Mary went into the garden with Mr Bassett and fed the rabbits and played with them, and after that they settled down to ludo.

By this time Miriam and Martyn and Mervyn

and Meg had finished writing and painting and cutting out and counting. They looked around for Mary-Mary, but she was nowhere to be seen. They looked upstairs and downstairs and all round the garden, but they couldn't find her anywhere. Then Miriam went out of the back door and found the note to the milkman inside the empty milk bottle. She read it, then she shouted to the others, and they all came running.

'She's gone away!' said Miriam.

'Where to?' said Martyn.

'Doesn't she say?' said Mervyn.

'How silly!' said Meg.

Then they all said together, 'Oh, dear! Whatever will Mother say?' And they began to get really worried.

They went down the road, looking in at the windows of all the shops and asking every one they knew. A boy was standing outside the sweetshop sucking a liquorice pipe.

'Have you seen a little girl come this way?' they asked him. 'With a bag?' 'And a hat?' 'And a pair of shoes?'

'Yes,' said the boy, 'and jolly funny she looked. Said she was going away to stay with a friend. She went into the old gent's house up there.'

Very relieved, they all went up the road again to Mr Bassett's house, the boy following them. He sat on the wall to watch what would happen, and Miriam, Martyn, Mervyn, and Meg rang the bell.

Mary-Mary opened the door. She looked very surprised to see them.

'You naughty girl!' they all said together. 'We've been looking for you everywhere.' 'Come home at once.' 'You shouldn't have gone away.'

Mary-Mary shut the door. Then she said through the letter-box, 'You shouldn't shout outside other people's houses. I'm ashamed of you.'

'Mary-Mary, you must come home!' called Miriam.

'No,' said Mary-Mary, 'you told me to go away, and I've gone away.'

'Open the door,' said Miriam.

'No,' said Mary-Mary.

'Where is Mr Bassett?' said Martyn.

'He's playing ludo and mustn't be disturbed,' said Mary-Mary.

'Let us in,' said Mervyn.

'No,' said Mary-Mary.

'Mother will be coming home soon,' said

"*Please* will you come back?"

Meg. 'You *must* come back. We're supposed to be looking after you.'

'I'm not coming back,' said Mary-Mary.

The others all whispered together in a worried sort of way, and the boy on the wall laughed rudely.

Then Miriam said, 'Mary-Mary, dear, I'm sorry we all told you to go away. Will you come back now?'

There was silence for a moment, then Mary-Mary opened the door.

'*Please* will you come back?' they said, all together.

Mary-Mary smiled.

'I don't think I'll come back,' she said, 'but I might come and stay with you if you ask me properly.'

'All right—please will you come and stay with us?'

'Will you treat me like a visitor?'

'We'll try,' they said.

'What will there be for tea?'

Miriam thought quickly and said, 'Sardine sandwiches.' (They were Mary-Mary's favourite.)

'Will you remember to say, "Take two as they're so small"?'

'Don't be silly,' said Miriam.

Mary-Mary started to shut the door again.

'I'm sorry I can't come and stay with you to-day,' she said. 'Perhaps some other time——'

But Martyn held the door open, and Miriam said, 'Yes, yes—take two as they're so small. Take three if you like. But do please come home—I mean, do please come and stay with us!'

'Very well,' said Mary-Mary; 'as you all want me so much, I'll come. But I must just go and pack my things. You can go on if you like and start getting tea ready for me.'

So Miriam, Martyn, Mervyn, and Meg went home (the boy on the wall laughed rudely as

—the boy on the wall laughed rudely

they went by), and Mary-Mary went and told Mr Bassett she was sorry she couldn't stay any longer, but her family very much wanted her to go and stay with them for a while.

She put on her shoes and her tea-cosy hat, and Mr Bassett saw her to the door.

On the doorstep she stopped to make sure she had got everything. She brought out the small bundle of comics.

'You might like to keep these,' she said. 'I brought them to read in bed, but I've got plenty more at home.'

'Thank you very much,' said Mr Bassett.

'And thank you for having me,' said Mary-Mary.

Miriam, Martyn, Mervyn, and Meg all came out to their own doorstep.

'Tea is nearly ready,' they called. 'We shall be so pleased if you will come.'

'Thank you, I will,' said Mary-Mary, and she set off down the steps.

The rude boy was still sitting on the wall.

'That was one up to you, wasn't it?' he said, laughing.

'I don't know what you mean,' said Mary-Mary.

'Go on!' said the boy. 'Of course you do. Everybody knows what "one up to you" means!'

'I'm sure *I* don't,' said Mary-Mary, and hobbled carefully up to her own front door, where all her big brothers and sisters were politely waiting for her.

So Mary-Mary went away and then came home again to stay, and that is the end of the story.

FIVE

Mary-Mary is a Surprise

One day Mary-Mary sat at the table giving Moppet his breakfast. She sat him beside her plate with one cornflake in front of his nose, and while she was waiting for him to eat it she listened to all her big brothers and sisters talking.

'Mrs Merry's party is going to be lovely,' said Miriam. 'It isn't going to end until half-past midnight.'

'Smashing,' said Martyn.

'Super,' said Mervyn.

'Golly!' said Meg.

'We've never been to such a late party before,' said Miriam. 'I suppose it's because it's a New Year party.'

'Whizzo,' said Martyn.

'Hooray,' said Mervyn.

'Gorgeous!' said Meg.

Mary-Mary was very surprised to hear that there was going to be a party.

'When are we going?' she asked.

But all the others said, 'No, not you, Mary-

Mary.' 'It's only us.' 'You weren't asked.' 'You're too little.'

Mary-Mary moved Moppet's nose a little closer to his cornflake and didn't say anything.

'Never mind,' said Miriam.

'Wait till you're bigger,' said Martyn.

'Then you'll be able to go too,' said Mervyn.

'If anyone asks you,' said Meg.

And they all said, 'Never mind, Mary-Mary,' together.

Mary-Mary got down from her place and said in a busy and rather worried voice, 'I couldn't have gone, anyway. I am far too busy. Moppet has a cold and he needs looking after.'

She gave a tiny sneeze in Moppet's voice and looked at the cornflake.

'You see, he hasn't even eaten his breakfast. I have to eat it for him.'

She put the cornflake in her mouth, then, still looking busy and worried, she carried Moppet away and put him to bed in a small cardboard box.

All the morning, while the others talked about the New Year party and what they should wear and who would fetch them home and what there would be to eat, Moppet's cold got worse and worse.

Mary-Mary sat with him and told him stories and tucked him up in cotton-wool and gave him medicine from a doll's tea-cup, and was so busy that she had no time at all to think about the party.

About an hour before dinner-time Mrs Merry came in on her way back from shopping. She was a fat, jolly lady whom they all liked; but as soon as Mary-Mary heard her voice in the hall she hid under the table with Moppet. She didn't want to see Mrs Merry to-day.

Miriam, Martyn, Mervyn, and Meg brought Mrs Merry into the dining-room, and they all started talking about the New Year party all over again.

'I have a lovely plan,' said Mrs Merry. 'I am going to dress Mr Merry up as a very old man, with a long white beard—to be the Old Year, you know. Then, when the clock strikes midnight (and it really is the end of the year), I thought how lovely it would be if we could have two or three fairies come in with a great big box of crackers to give away to everybody to wish them a Happy New Year.'

'Fairies?' said Meg.

'Not real fairies,' said Mrs Merry, 'and that's what I've come about. I wanted to ask you if

you'd like to help. We shall need quite big
people, because I'm planning to have a really
huge box of crackers. Now, how would you like
to be the fairies?'

'Oh, yes!' said Miriam.

'What—me?' said Martyn.

'Oh, no!' said Mervyn.

'Oh, *yes*!' said Meg.

'No, not you boys,' said Mrs Merry. 'I meant
Miriam and Meg.'

Martyn and Mervyn looked relieved, and
Miriam and Meg were delighted.

'But what shall we wear?' they said.

Mrs Merry said she had two fairy dresses that
would just fit them.

'They used to belong to Barbara and Bunty,'
she said, 'but the dresses are too small now, and,
anyway, Barbara and Bunty have grown too fat
to be fairies any more—so we thought it would
be lovely if you two would do it. But don't tell
anyone. It is to be a surprise.'

Mary-Mary, under the table, said to Moppet, 'Shall I tell you a story? Once upon a time
there were two huge great fairies ——'

'Mary-Mary!' said Miriam. 'Go away at
once. You shouldn't have been listening.'

'—and their names both began with an
M——' went on Mary-Mary.

"Once upon a time there were two huge great fairies"

'Oh, do go away!' said Miriam and Meg.

'—and they were called Margarine and Marmalade——' said Mary-Mary.

'Shall we push her out?' said Martyn.

'Take me away!' said Mary-Mary in Moppet's voice. 'I don't believe in fairies—I only believe in mice.'

Mary-Mary crawled out from under the table, saying to Moppet, 'Very well, I'll take you away and tell you a mouse story.' And she went into the kitchen where Mother was busy cooking the dinner.

Mary-Mary sat under the draining-board and told Moppet his mouse story, which went like this, 'Once upon a time there was a poor little mouse who had a very bad cold, and it got worse and worse, until somebody gave him an ice-cream, and then all of a sudden it got better.'

Mother looked up from her cooking.

'How bad is Moppet's cold now?' she asked.

'It is a bit worse,' said Mary-Mary, 'but I don't think he'll die of it—at least, not yet—at least, I *hope* not.'

'Do you think an ice-cream would help him?' asked Mother.

'Oh, yes,' said Mary-Mary. 'What a good idea!'

So Mother gave her threepence, and Mary-Mary ran down to the shop and bought an ice-cream. On the way back she saw Mrs Merry coming down the road.

'I mustn't stop and talk to her,' said Mary-Mary to herself. 'I must hurry home to my poor child, Moppet, who has such a nasty cold. I will talk to her another day.'

So she put her head down and began to run. She was hoping that if she ran fast enough Mrs Merry wouldn't have time to see who it was. But Mrs Merry called out, 'Why, Mary-Mary! You're just the person I want to see.' So Mary-Mary had to stop, after all.

"I must hurry home to my poor child, Moppet."

'You heard all about the plan for my party, didn't you?' said Mrs Merry. 'Well, I'm planning a surprise at the end that I didn't tell the others about. I need some one very little to help me do it, and you're just the person I want. Now, will you come to my party secretly, without anyone knowing? Mr Merry will fetch you in the car while the party is going on. I have a lovely dress for you to wear, and I want you to come as the big surprise when the clock strikes midnight. Do you think you would like to be the surprise at my party?'

'Oh, yes!' said Mary-Mary. 'I've quite often

been a surprise by mistake, but it would be very nice to be a surprise on purpose.'

'I've asked your mother,' said Mrs Merry, 'and she says it will be quite all right. She knows all about it and she's not going to tell any of the others; so you mustn't either. Come to tea with me to-day, and we will plan it together.'

Mary-Mary ran home feeling very pleased indeed. Moppet's ice-cream was nearly melted by the time she got there, so she gave it to him in a tea-cup. She sang so loudly while she was helping him to eat it that Miriam, Martyn, Mervyn, and Meg were quite surprised.

'Why is Mary-Mary so happy all of a sudden?' they said.

'Mrs Merry has asked her to tea to-day,' said Mother.

'Oh, because she can't go to the party!' they said.

'Is Moppet's cold better now?' asked Mother.

'Quite, quite better,' said Mary-Mary, licking up the last of the ice-cream. 'I knew it would be.'

When New Year's Eve came Miriam, Martyn, Mervyn, and Meg were all very excited. Mary-Mary watched them getting ready for the party and tried not to look excited too.

She went to bed in her underclothes, with a

nightie on top so that the others wouldn't guess. (She was going to have supper on a tray when they had gone, and Mother had promised to read her a story until it was time for Mr Merry to come and fetch her.)

When they were ready to go Miriam, Martyn, Mervyn, and Meg all came to say good-night to her. Mary-Mary hid under the blankets, because she couldn't help laughing, and they thought she was hiding because she was sad about not going to the party. So they were all very kind to her.

'Never mind, Mary-Mary,' they said. 'When you're bigger you will be able to go to a New Year party too.'

Miriam said, 'Don't cry. I'll give you one of my party hair ribbons to-morrow.'

Martyn said, 'Cheer up, and I'll bring you back something nice to eat.'

Mervyn said, 'I'll save you my paper serviette. It will make a tablecloth for Moppet.'

And Meg said, 'Go to sleep now, like a good girl, and I'll tell you all about it in the morning.'

Mary-Mary (still under the blankets) said, 'Thank you' and 'Good-bye' and 'Have a nice time'; and then off they all went.

It was a lovely party. Miriam, Martyn, Mervyn, and Meg had a very jolly time.

A little while before midnight Miriam and Meg slipped away to put on their fairy clothes. As they ran through the hall on their way upstairs they saw Mr Merry just coming in at the front door with a great big round box in his arms.

'Hallo!' he said. 'Are you having a good time?'

'Oh, yes!' they said, both together.

'And where are the rest of your family?' asked Mr Merry.

'Martyn and Mervyn are in the sitting-room with the others,' said Miriam.

'And Mary-Mary is fast asleep in bed,' said Meg.

'Why?' said Mr Merry. 'Has she been naughty?'

'Oh, no!' said Miriam and Meg together, 'but she's *much* too little to come to a New Year party.'

'You two are going to be the fairies, aren't you?' said Mr Merry.

'Yes,' they said. 'Are those the crackers in that box? Can we see?'

'Not to be opened till midnight!' said Mr Merry, laughing. 'You will be careful not to drop it, won't you? It is heavier than you might think.'

He carried the box into the kitchen and shut the door, and Miriam and Meg ran on upstairs to change.

In the sitting-room Martyn and Mervyn were very busy. Mrs Merry had put them in charge of the games (with Billy and Bob to help them) while she went away to see to one or two things. Barbara and Bunty were seeing to the refreshments.

They had just finished a game of Blind Man's Buff when Mrs Merry came back, looking very jolly.

'What time is it?' she asked.

'It's nearly midnight!' shouted all the children, pointing at the clock.

'So it is!' said Mrs Merry. 'Now, stand back, all of you, and make a way through. I believe I hear some one coming.'

Every one stood back. Then the door opened and in came a very old man with a long white beard. He limped across the room, leaning heavily on a stick, and peered up at the clock.

'Who is he?' somebody whispered.

Every one started talking at once. 'I know! He's the Old Year!' 'How wonderful!' 'And he's looking at the clock, because he's only got

—carrying a large round box between them

another minute left!' (But hardly anyone
guessed it was really Mr Merry dressed up.)

As the clock began striking twelve the old
man turned and hobbled out of the room. At
the same minute there was the sound of bells
ringing, and two fairies came running in, carrying a large round box between them. They
looked so pretty in their pink-and-blue dresses
with silver wings that every one started clapping
and saying, 'Oh, aren't they lovely!' (But

hardly anyone guessed it was really Miriam and Meg.)

The fairies put the big box down on the floor and smiled and curtseyed. Then, on the last stroke of twelve, they bent down and lifted the lid.

'OH!' cried every one, 'Oh, just look! How *sweet*!' For there, rising out of the box with her arms full of crackers, was the sweetest little fairy person. She was wearing a short frock and a silver crown with a star on her head.

'It's the little New Year!' they all cried. 'Oh, *isn't* she sweet? What a lovely idea! Who can she be?'

And, of course, it was Mary-Mary!

'Happy New Year, everybody!' she called, and, climbing out of the box, she threw the crackers to every one.

Miriam and Meg, as well as Martyn and Mervyn, could hardly believe their eyes.

'It's Mary-Mary!' they all said. 'However did she get here?' 'We left her at home in bed!' 'But doesn't she look pretty!'

And after a while, when they had stopped being quite so surprised, they began to feel rather proud of Mary-Mary.

Every one began asking who the sweet little girl really was, and Miriam, Martyn, Mervyn,

and Meg wandered around saying, 'Oh, that's our little sister, Mary-Mary.'

'Didn't you know she was coming?' some one asked.

'No,' they said. 'We *were* surprised. Yes, she is rather sweet, isn't she? We're quite proud of her.'

Mary-Mary, sitting on Mrs Merry's lap, eat-

ing a chocolate ice-cream, heard all this and
smiled to herself. She was rather surprised too.

*So Mary-Mary did go to the New Year party
after all, and that is the end of the story.*

More Mary-Mary

JOAN G. ROBINSON

Mary-Mary likes to make 'interesting' things happen. So she locks herself in the bathroom. Four firemen, in their helmets and big black boots come to let her out. And then they stay to tea!

Mary-Mary is too young to go to the garden party on her own. So she dresses up in her lady's dress, battered hat and best handbag – and suddenly she's Miss Muffin, who is *certainly* old enough to take care of herself! And so is Mary-Mary!

Mary-Mary is also an Armada Lion.

Along Came a Dog

MEINDERT DEJONG

The little red hen was different from all the other hens in
the barnyard, and that made her an outcast. She was cocky
and mean, but she needed protection. At least that's what
the big black dog thought. So he became her slave. He was
at the little hen's beck and call. With a swipe of his paw
he sent her enemy, the weasel, packing! And a growl drove
the squawking rooster away in terror!

He stole eggs from the other hens for her to sit on. Then
one day she had five little chicks. The big black dog had a
family at last!

Catherine Storr

LUCY
LUCY RUNS AWAY

'I wish I was a boy,' said Lucy. 'Boys are stronger. They have bicycles and real fights. Boys have adventures.' When the boys in the neighbourhood refuse to let her join their gang, Lucy is even more determined to prove her bravery. 'I shall be a detective. I shall walk around and find some terrible crime going on. I am Lew the Fabulous Detective.' But no one was more surprised than Lucy when she caught a thief. This adventure is told in *Lucy*.

In *Lucy Runs Away* eager for further adventures Lucy decides to leave home when she turns eight. So with a satchel bulging and her savings in her pocket, she sets off to the seaside as the Mysterious Outlaw.

Perfect stories for seven-year-olds and upwards.

The Paddington Books

MICHAEL BOND

Paddington is a *very* rare bear indeed! He'd travelled all the way from darkest Peru (with only a jar of marmalade a suitcase and his hat) when the Brown family first met him on Paddington Station. Since then their lives have never been quite the same . . . for things just seem to *happen* to Paddington—chaotic things . . .

What *other* bear could turn his friend's wedding into an uproar by getting the wedding ring stuck on his paw? Or glue himself to his dancing partner's back with his marmalade sandwich? *Only* Paddington . . . but as he says himself, 'Oh dear, I'm in trouble again.'

'Within a comparatively short time, Paddington has joined Pooh as one of the great bears of children's literature.'

The Teacher

Paddington's own particular brand of chaos comes up often in Armada Lions—in *A Bear Called Paddington*, *More About Paddington*, *Paddington Goes to Town*, *Paddington Helps Out*, *Paddington at Large*, *Paddington Abroad* and *Paddington Takes the Air*.